Redruff
the Partridge of Don Valley

By Ernest Thompson Seton

Retold by Quinn Currie

Illustrated by Susan Heinonen

ISBN 1-880812-15-0

Published by Storytellers Ink
Seattle, Washington

Printed in the United States of America

PROLOGUE

This story is true. Although I have left the strict line of
historical truth in many places, the animals in this book
were all real characters. They lived the lives I have depicted,
and showed the stamp of heroism and personality more
strongly by far than it has been in the power of my pen to tell.

Redruff really lived in the Don Valley north of Toronto,
and many of my companions will remember him.

– Ernest Thompson Seton

JANUARY

Stormy Moon

FEBRUARY

Hungry Moon

MARCH

Wakening Moon

APRIL

Pussy-willow Moon

DECEMBER

Snow Moon

CONTENTS

MAY

Love Moon

Chapter I	Mother and the Fox	1
Chapter II	Learning to Fly	10
Chapter III	The Hunter	18
Chapter IV	Coming of Age	23
Chapter V	Wintertime	27
Chapter VI	Redruff the Father	36
Chapter VII	The Gunner Moon	53

NOVEMBER

Migrating Moon

JUNE

Chick Moon

OCTOBER

Acorn Moon

SEPTEMBER

Gunner Moon

AUGUST

Molting Moon

JULY

Berry Moon

Chapter I
Fooling the Fox

The Mother Partridge led her brood down the wooded slope of Taylor's Hill; toward the crystal brook that by some strange whim was called Mud Creek. Her little ones were one day old but already quick of foot, and she was taking them for their first drink.

She walked slowly, crouching low as she went, for the woods were full of enemies. She uttered a soft little cluck in her throat, a call to the balls of down that came toddling after her on tiny pink legs. They peeped softly and plaintively if left even a few inches behind, and looked so fragile they would make a chickadee appear big and coarse.

There were twelve of them, and Mother Grouse watched them all; and she watched every bush and tree and thicket, and the whole woods and the sky itself. She watched for enemies constantly and on this day she found one.

1

Away across the level beaver meadow a fox was approaching in their direction and in a few moments would surely catch their scent or strike their trail. There was no time to lose.

'*Krrr! Krr!*' (Hide! Hide!) cried the mother in a low firm voice, and the little bits of things, scarcely bigger than acorns and but a day old, scattered far (a few inches) apart to hide. One dove under a leaf, another between two roots, a third crawled into a curl of birchbark, a fourth into a hole, and so on, until all were hidden but one, who could find no cover and so squatted on a broad yellow chip, lay very flat, and closed his eyes tight, sure that now he was safe from being seen. They ceased their frightened peeping and all was silent.

Mother Partridge flew straight toward the dreaded fox, alighted fearlessly a few yards to one side of him, and then flung herself on the ground, flopping, dragging one wing and lame – oh, so dreadfully lame – and whining like a distressed puppy. Was she begging for mercy – mercy from a fox? Oh, no! She was too smart for that. She was well aware of the cleverness of the fox.

Clever or not, he was no match for a mother partridge. Elated at the prize so suddenly within his reach, the fox turned with a dash and caught – at least, no, he didn't quite catch the bird; she flopped by chance just a foot out of reach. He followed with another jump and would have seized her this time surely, but somehow a sapling came just between, and the partridge dragged herself awkwardly away and under a log, but the great brute snapped his jaws and bounded over the log, while she, seeming a trifle less lame, made another clumsy forward spring and tumbled down a bank, and the fox, keenly following, almost caught her tail, but, oddly enough, fast as he went and leaped, she still seemed just a trifle faster.

It was most extraordinary. An injured partridge and he, Swift-foot the fox, had not caught her in five minutes' racing. It was really shameful. But the partridge seemed to gain strength as the fox put forth his, and after a quarter of a mile race, all leading somehow away from Taylor's Hill, the bird got unaccountably quite well, and, rising with a derisive whirr, flew off through the woods leaving the fox utterly dumfounded to realize that he had been fooled, and, worst of all, he now realized that this was not the first time he had been served this very trick, though he never guessed the reason.

Meanwhile Mother Partridge skimmed in a great circle and came by a roundabout way back to the little fuzz-balls she had left hidden in the woods.

With a wild bird's keen memory for places, she went to the very grass-blade she last trod on, and stood for a moment fondly to admire the perfect stillness of her children. Even at her step not one had stirred, and the little fellow on the chip, not so badly concealed after all, had not budged, nor did he now; he only closed his eyes a tiny little bit harder, till the mother said:

'K-reet!' (Come, children) and instantly like a fairy story, every hole gave up its little baby partridge, and the wee fellow on the chip, the biggest of them all really, opened his big-little eyes and ran to the shelter of her broad tail, with a little 'peep peep' which an enemy could not have heard three feet away, but which his mother could not have missed thrice as far. All the other thimblefuls of down joined in, and probably thought themselves dreadfully noisy, and were proportionately happy.

5

The sun was hot now. There was an open space to cross on the road to the water, and, after a careful lookout for enemies, the mother gathered the little things under the shadow of her spread fantail and kept off all danger of sunstroke until they reached the brier thicket by the stream.

Here a cottontail rabbit leaped out and gave them a great scare. But the flag of truce he carried behind was enough.

He was an old friend; and among other things the little ones learned that day that rabbit always sails under a flag of truce, and lives up to it too.

And then came the drink. At first the little fellows didn't know how, but they copied their mother, and soon learned. There they stood in a row along the edge, twelve little brown and golden balls on twenty-four little pink-toed, in-turned feet, with twelve sweet little golden heads gravely bowing and drinking.

Then she led them by short stages, keeping under cover, to the far side of the beaver-meadow, to a large grassy dome which she had noticed some time before. It takes a number of such domes to raise a brood of partridges.

It was an ant's nest. The mother stepped on top and gave half a dozen vigorous rakes with her claws. The ant hill was broken open, and the earthen galleries scattered in ruins down the slope. The ants swarmed out and quarreled with each other for lack of a better plan. Some ran around the hill with vast energy and little purpose, while a few of the more sensible began to carry away fat white eggs.

But the mother partridge, coming to the little ones, picked up one of these juicy-looking bags and clucked and dropped it, and picked it up again and again and clucked, then swallowed it. The young ones stood around, then one little yellow fellow, the one that sat on the chip, picked up an ant egg, dropped it a few times, then yielding to a sudden impulse, swallowed it, and so had learned to eat.

Within twenty minutes even the runt had learned, and a merry time they had scrambling after the delicious eggs as their mother broke open more ant galleries, and sent them and their contents rolling down the bank, till every little partridge had so crammed his crop that he was positively misshapen and could eat no more.

Then all went cautiously up the stream, and on a sandy bank, well screened by brambles, they lay all that afternoon, and learned how pleasant it was to feel the cool powdery dust running between their toes. With their strong bent for copying, they lay on their sides like their mother and scratched with their tiny feet and flopped with their wings, though they had no wings to flop with, only a little tag in the down on each side, to show where the wings would come.

That night she took them to a dry thicket near by, and there amongst the crisp, dead leaves that would prevent an enemy's silent approach on foot, and under the interlacing briers that kept off all foes of the air, she cradled them in their feather-shingled nursery and rejoiced in the fullness of a mother's joy over her babies as they peeped in their sleep and snuggled so trustfully against her warm body.

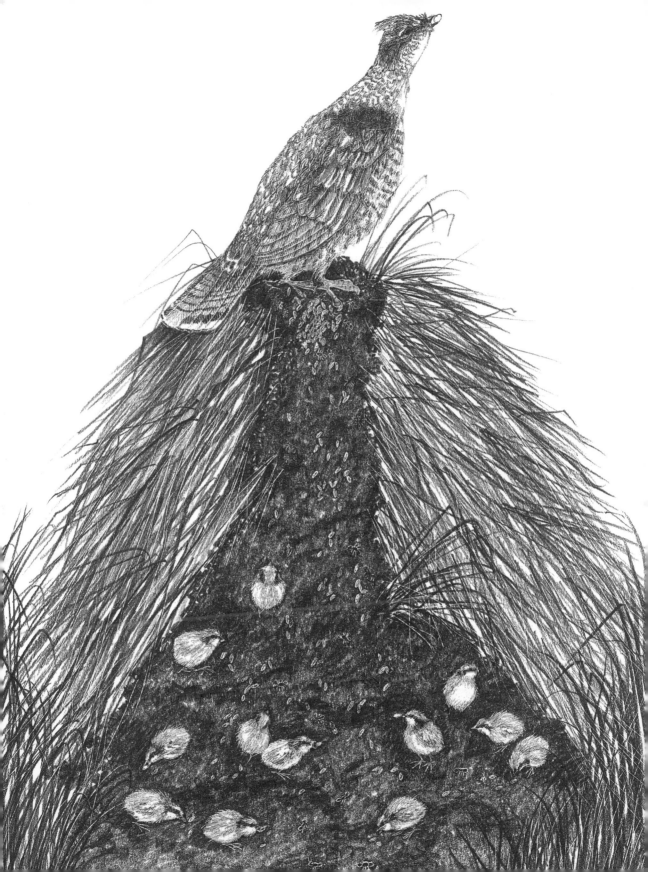

Chapter II
Learning to Fly

The third day the chicks were much stronger on their feet. They no longer had to go around an acorn; they could even scramble over pine cones, and on the little tags that marked the places for their wings, were now to be seen blue rows of quills.

Their start in life was a good mother, good legs and a few reliable instincts. It was instinct which taught them to hide at a word from their mother, and to obey her instantly.

Next day the quills had sprouted the tips of feathers. On the next, the feathers were well out, and a week later the whole family of down-clad babies were strong on the wing.

And yet not all – the little runt had been sickly from the first. He bore his half-shell on his back for hours after he came out; he ran less and cheeped more than his brothers, and when one evening at the onset of a skunk the mother gave the word '*Kwit, kwit*' (Fly, fly), Runtie was left behind, and when she gathered her brood on the piney hill he was missing, and they saw him no more.

Meanwhile, their training had gone on. They knew that the finest grasshoppers were in the long grass by the brook; they knew that the currant bushes dropped smooth, green worms; they knew that the dome of an ant hill held good things to eat; they knew that strawberries, though not really insects, were almost as delicious; they knew that the huge butterflies were good, safe game, if they could only catch them, and that a slab of bark dropping from the side of a rotten log was sure to abound in good things; and they also learned that yellow-jackets, mud wasps, woolly worms, and hundred-leggers were better left alone.

It was now July, the Moon of Berries. The chicks had grown and flourished amazingly during this last month, and were now so large that in her efforts to cover them the mother was kept standing all night.

They took their daily dust bath, but had changed to one higher on the hill. It was in use by many different birds, and at first the mother disliked the idea of such a second-hand bath. But the dust was of such a fine agreeable quality, that she forgot her mistrust.

Soon after, the little ones began to droop and she herself did not feel well. They were always hungry, and though they ate more than enough, they grew thinner. The mother was the last to be affected. But when it came, it came hard – a ravenous hunger, a feverish headache, and a wasting weakness. She never knew the cause.

Eventually, the sickness passed. But not for all of them. The weakest, by inexorable law, dropped out. Enfeebled by the disease, they drank and drank by the stream, and the next morning did not move when the others followed the mother.

Seven little partridges now obeyed the mother's call. Their individual characters were shown early and now developed fast. The weaklings were gone, but there were still a fool and lazy one. The mother could not help caring for some more than for others, and her favorite was the biggest, he who once sat on the yellow chip for concealment. He was not only the biggest and strongest of the brood, but best of all, the most obedient. His mother's warning *'rrrrr'* (danger) did not always keep the others from a risky path or a doubtful food, but obedience seemed natural to him, and he never failed to respond to her soft *'K-reet'* (Come), and of this obedience he reaped the reward, for his life would be the longest.

August, the Molting Moon, went by; the young ones were now three parts grown. They knew just enough to think themselves wonderfully wise. When they were small it was necessary to sleep on the ground so their mother could shelter them, but now they were too big to need that, and the mother began to introduce grown-up ways of life. It was time to roost in the trees. The young weasels, foxes, skunks, and minks were beginning to run. The ground grew more and more dangerous each night, so at sundown Mother Partridge called *'K-reet,'* and flew into a thick, low tree.

The little ones followed, except one, who persisted in sleeping on the ground as before. It was all right that time, but the next night his brothers were awakened by his cries. There was a slight scuffle, then stillness. They peered down into the terrible darkness below, where the glint of two close-set eyes and a peculiar musty smell told them that a mink had made off with their brother.

Six little partridges now sat in a row at night, with their mother in the middle, though it was not unusual for some little one with cold feet to perch on her back.

Their education went on, and about this time they were taught 'whirring.' A partridge can rise on the wing silently if it wishes, but whirring is so important at times that all are taught how and when to rise on thundering wings. Many ends are gained by the whirr. It warns all other partridges near that danger is at hand, it unnerves the gunner, or it fixes the foe's attention on the whirrer, while the others sneak off in silence, or by squatting, escape notice.

September came, with seeds and grain in place of berries and ant eggs, and gunners in place of skunks and mink.

The partridges knew well what a fox was, but had scarcely seen a dog. They knew they could easily baffle a fox by taking to a tree, but when in the Gunner Moon old man Clyde came prowling through the ravine with his bob-tailed yellow cur, the mother spied the dog and cried out, 'Kwit! kwit!' (Fly, fly). Two of the brood thought it a pity their mother should lose her wits so easily over a fox, and were pleased to show their superior nerve by springing into a tree in spite of her earnestly repeated 'Kwit! kwit!' and her example of speeding away on silent wings.

Meanwhile, the strange bob-tailed fox came under the tree and yapped and yapped at them. They were much amused at him and at their mother and brothers, so much so that they never noticed a rustling in the bushes till there was a loud *Bang! bang!* and down fell two partridges, to be seized by the yellow cur until the hunter ran from the bushes and took them.

17

Chapter III
The Hunter

Clyde lived in a wretched shanty near the Don, north of Toronto. His was what some would call an ideal existence. He had no money, no taxes, no social pretensions, and no property to speak of. His life was made up of a very little work and a great deal of play, with as much outdoor life as he chose. The neighbors called him a squatter, and looked on him merely as an anchored tramp. He shot and trapped the year round, and varied his game somewhat with the season, but had been heard to remark he could tell the month by the 'taste of the partridges,' if he didn't happen to know by the almanac. This, no doubt, showed keen observation, but was also unfortunate proof of something not so credible. The lawful season for hunting partridges began September 15th, but there was nothing surprising in Clyde's being out two weeks ahead of time. Yet he managed to escape the game warden year after year.

He rarely shot on the wing, preferring to shoot a sitting bird, which was not easy to do when the leaves were on, and accounted for the brood going so long unharmed; but the near prospect of other gunners finding them now had stirred him to go after 'a mess o' birds.' He had heard no roar of wings when the mother bird led off her four survivors, so pocketed the two he had shot and returned to the shanty.

The little grouse thus learned that a dog is not a fox, and must be differently played; and an old lesson was yet more deeply graven: 'Obedience is long life.'

The partridges spent the rest of September keeping quietly out of the way of gunners as well as some old enemies. They still roosted on the long thin branches of the hardwood trees among the thickest leaves, which protected them from foes on the air; the height saved them from foes on the ground, and left them nothing to fear but raccoons, whose slow, heavy tread on the limber boughs never failed to give them timely warning. But the leaves were falling now. This was nut time, and it was owl time, too.

Barred owls coming down from the north doubled or tripled the owl population. The nights were getting frosty and the raccoons less dangerous, so the mother changed the place of roosting to the thickest foliage of a hemlock tree.

Only one of the brood disregarded the warning '*Kreet, kreet.*' He stuck to his swinging elm bough, now nearly naked, and a great yellow-eyed owl bore him off before morning.

Mother and three young ones now were left, but they were as big as she was; indeed one, the eldest, he of the chip, was bigger. Their ruffs had begun to show. Just the tips, to tell what they would be like when grown, and very proud they were of them.

The ruff is to the partridge what the train is to the peacock – his chief beauty and his pride. A hen's ruff is black with a slight green gloss. Once in a while a partridge is born of unusual size and vigor, whose ruff is not only larger, but by a peculiar kind of intensification is of a deep coppery red, iridescent with violet, green, and gold. Such a bird is sure to be a wonder to all who know him, and the little one who had squatted on the chip, and had always done what he was told, developed before the Acorn Moon had changed, into all the glory of a gold and copper ruff – for this was Redruff, the famous partridge of the Don Valley.

Chapter IV
Coming of Age

One day late in the Acorn Moon, that is, about mid-October, as the grouse family were basking near a great pine log on the sunlit edge of the beaver-meadow, they heard the far-away bang of a gun, and Redruff, acting on some impulse from within, leaped on the log, strutted up and down a couple of times, then, yielding to the elation of the bright, clean, bracing air, he whirred his wings in loud defiance. Then, giving fuller vent to this expression of vigor, just as a colt frisks to show how well he feels, he whirred yet more loudly, until, suddenly, he found himself drumming, and tickled with the discovery of his new power, thumped the air again and again till he filled the near woods with the loud tattoo of the fully grown partridge. His brother and sister heard and looked on with admiration and surprise; so did his mother.

In early November comes the moon of change. By a strange law
of nature, all partridges fly off in the November moon of their first year.
They become possessed with a desire to get away somewhere, it does
not matter much where. They go drifting over the country by night, and
daylight finds them in all sorts of places, in open marshes or even perched
on telephone wires in the city. The desire to move seems to be a bygone
habit of migration, and has one good effect, it breaks up the families and
prevents the constant intermating, which would surely be fatal to their race.
It always happens to the young their first year, and they may do it again the
second fall; but in the third season it is practically unknown.

Redruff's mother knew it was coming as soon as she saw the frost
grapes blackening, and the maples shedding their crimson and gold leaves.
There was nothing to do but care for them and keep them in the quietest part
of the woods.

The first sign of the great restlessness came when a flock of wild geese went *honking* southward overhead. The young ones had never before seen such long-necked hawks, and were afraid of them. But seeing that their mother had no fear, they took courage, and watched them with intense interest. Was it the wild, clanging cry that moved them, or was it solely instinct?

A strange longing to follow took possession of each of the young ones. They watched those geese fading away to the south, and sought out higher perches to watch them farther still, and from that time things were not the same. The November moon was waxing, and when it was full, the November desire came.

The least vigorous of the flock were the most affected. The little family was scattered. Redruff himself flew on several long erratic night journeys. The impulse took him southward, but there lay the boundless stretch of Lake Ontario, so he turned again, and the waning of the Migration Moon found him once more in the Mud Creek Glen, but absolutely alone.

Chapter V
Wintertime

Food grew scarce as winter wore on. Redruff clung to the old ravine and the piney sides of Taylor's Hill, and every month brought its food and foes. The Migrating Moon brought travel, solitude, and grapes; the Snow Moon came with rosehips; and the Stormy Moon brought browse of birch and silver storms that sheathed the woods in ice, and made it hard to keep one's perch while pulling off the frozen buds.

Redruff's beak grew terribly worn with the work, so that even when closed there was still an opening through behind the hook. But nature had prepared him for the slippery footing; his toes, so slim and trim in September, had sprouted rows of sharp, horny points, and these grew with the growing cold, till the first snow had found him fully equipped with snow-shoes and ice-creepers. The cold weather had driven away most of the hawks and owls, and made it impossible for his four-footed enemies to approach unseen, so that his life was nearly balanced.

His daily flight in search of food led him farther and farther, till he had discovered and explored the Rosedale Creek, with its banks of silver birch, and Castle Frank, with its grapes and berries, as well as Chester woods, where Virginia creeper swung their fruit clusters, and checkerberries glowed beneath the snow.

He soon found that for some reason men with guns did not go within the high fence of Castle Frank. So among these woons he lived his life, learning new places, new foods, and grew wiser and more beautiful every day.

He was quite alone so far as kindred were concerned, but that scarcely seemed a hardship. Wherever he went he could see the jolly chickadees scrambling merrily about, and he remembered the time when they had seemed such big, important birds. They were the most absurdly cheerful creatures in the woods.

Before autumn was fairly over they had begun to sing their famous refrain, *'Spring Soon,'* and kept it up with good heart more or less all through the winter's direst storms, till at length the waning of the Hungry Moon, February, seemed really to lend some point to the ditty, and they redoubled their optimistic announcement to the world in an 'I-told-you-so' mood.

Soon the sun gained strength and melted the snow from the southern slope of Castle Frank hill, and exposed great banks of fragrant wintergreen, whose berries were a bounteous feast for Redruff, and, ending the hard work of pulling frozen browse, gave his bill the needed chance to grow into its proper shape again. Very soon the first bluebird came flying over and warbled as he flew *'Spring is coming.'* The sun kept gaining, and early one day in the dark of the Wakening Moon of March there was a loud *'Caw, caw,'* and old Silverspot, the king crow, came swinging along from the south at the head of his troops and officially announced

'THE SPRING HAS COME.'

All nature seemed to respond to this, the opening of the bird's New Year, and yet it was something within that chiefly seemed to move them. The chickadees went simply wild; they sang their *'Spring now, spring now now – Spring now now,'* so persistently that one wondered how they found the time to get a living.

And Redruff felt it thrill him through and through. He sprang with joyous vigor on a stump and sent rolling down the little valley, again and again, a thundering *'Thump, thump, thump, thunderrrrrrrrr,'* that wakened dull echoes as it rolled, and voiced his gladness in the coming of spring.

Away down the valley was Clyde's shanty. He heard the drum-call on the still morning air and 'reckoned there was a partridge to git,' and came sneaking up the ravine with his gun. But Redruff skimmed away in silence, nor rested till once more in Mud Creek Glen. And there he mounted the very log where first he had drummed and rolled his loud tattoo again and again.

Why does a happy boy shout? Why does a lonesome youth sigh? They don't know any more than Redruff knew why every day now he mounted some dead log and thumped and thundered to the woods; then strutted and admired his gorgeous blazing ruffs as they flashed their jewels in the sunlight, and then thundered out again. Whence now came the strange wish for someone else to admire the plumes? And why had such a notion never come till the Pussywillow Moon?

'Thump, thump, thunder-r-r-r-r-rrrr'
'Thump, thump, thunder-r-r-r-r-rrrr'
he rumbled again and again.

Day after day he sought the favorite log, and a new beauty, a rose-red comb, grew out above each clear, keen eye, and the clumsy snow shoes were wholly shed from his feet. His ruff grew finer, his eyes brighter, and his whole appearance splendid to behold, as he strutted and flashed in the sun. But now he was what? He didn't quite understand that it was *lonesome*.

Yet what could he do but blindly vent his hankering in this daily drum parade, till on a day early in May, when the trilliums had fringed his log with silver stars, and he had drummed and longed, then drummed again, his keen ear caught a sound, a gentle footfall in the brush. He turned to a statue and watched; he knew he had been watched. Could it be possible?

Yes! there it was – a form – a shy little lady grouse, now bashfully seeking to hide. In a moment he was by her side. His whole nature swamped by a new feeling – burnt up with thirst – a cooling spring in sight. And how he spread and flashed his proud array! How came he to know that that would please?

He puffed his plumes and contrived to stand just right to catch the sun, and strutted and uttered a low, soft chuckle that must have been just as good as the 'sweet nothings' of another race, for clearly now her heart was won. Won, really, days ago, if only he had known. For full three days she had come at the loud tattoo and coyly admired him from afar, and felt a little piqued that he had not yet found her, so close at hand. So it was not quite all chance, perhaps, that little stamp that caught his ear. But now she meekly bowed her head with sweet grace.

Oh, those were bright, glad days in the lovely glen. The sun was never so bright, and the piny air was balmier sweet than dreams. And the great noble bird came daily on his log, sometimes with her and sometimes quite alone and drummed for very joy of being alive.

But why sometimes alone? Why not forever with his brownie bride? Why should she stay to feast and play with him for hours, then take some stealthy chance to slip away and see him no more for hours or till next day? There was a woodland mystery here he could not solve. Why should her stay with him grow daily less till it was down to minutes, and one day at last she never came at all. Nor the next, nor the next, and Redruff, wild, careened on lightning wing and drummed on the old log, then away upstream on another log, and skimmed the hill to another ravine to drum and drum.

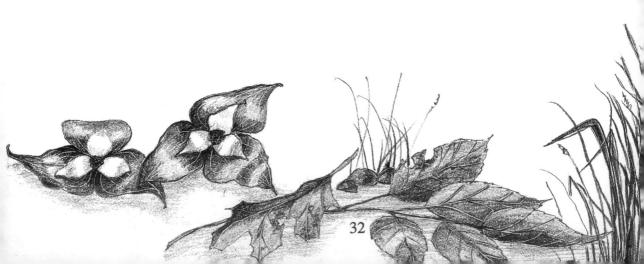

But on the fourth day, when he came and loudly called her, as of old, at their earliest tryst, he heard a sound in the bushes, as at first, and there was his missing Brownie bride with ten little peeping partridges following after.

Redruff skimmed to her side, frightening the bright-eyed downlings, and joined the brood he was to care for as his father never had for him.

Chapter VI
Redruff the Father

Good fathers are rare in the grouse world. The mother grouse builds her nest and hatches out her young without help. She even hides the place of the nest from the father and meets him only at the drum log and the feeding ground, or perhaps the dusting place, which is the clubhouse of the grouse.

When Brownie's little ones came out they had filled her every thought, even to the forgetting of their splendid father. But on the third day, when they were strong enough, she had taken them with her at the father's call.

Some fathers take no interest in their little ones, but Redruff joined in at once to help Brownie in the task of rearing the brood. They had learned to eat and drink just as their father had learned long ago, and could toddle along, with their mother leading the way, while the father ranged nearby or followed far behind.

The very next day, as they went from the hillside down toward the creek in a somewhat drawn out string, like beads with a big one at each end, a red squirrel, peaking around a pine trunk, watched the procession of downlings with the runtie straggling far in the rear. Redruff, yards behind, preening his feathers on a high log, had escaped the eye of the squirrel, whose strange desire for bird was roused at what seemed so fair a chance. With evil intent to cut off the hindmost straggler, he made a dash. Brownie could not have seen him until too late, but Redruff did. He flew for that red haired cutthroat; his weapons were his fists, that is, the knob-joints of the wings, and what a blow he could strike! At the first onset he struck the squirrel square on the end of the nose, his weakest spot, and sent him reeling; he staggered and wriggled into a brush pile, where he had expected to carry the little grouse, and there lay gasping with red drops trickling down his snout. The partridges left him lying there, and what became of him they never knew, but he troubled them no more.

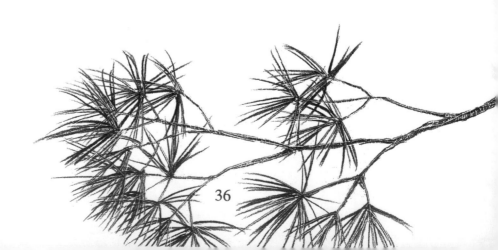

The family went on toward the water, but a cow had left deep tracks in the sandy loam, and one of the chicks fell and peeped in dire distress when he found he could not get out.

This was a problem. Neither parent seemed to know what to do, but as they trampled vainly round the edge, the sandy bank caved in, and, running down, formed a long slope, up which the young one ran and rejoined his brothers under the broad veranda of their mother's tail.

Brownie was a bright little mother, of small stature, but keen of wit and sense, and was, night and day, alert to care for her darling chicks. How proudly she stepped and clucked through the arching woods with her dainty brood behind her; how she strained her little brown tail almost half-circle to give them a broader shade, and never flinched at sight of any foe, but held ready to fight or fly, whichever seemed the best for her little ones.

Before the chicks could fly they had a meeting with old Clyde; though it was June, he was out with his gun. He went up the third ravine, and Tike, his dog, ranging ahead, came so dangerously near the Brownie brood that Redruff ran to meet him and by the old but never failing trick led him on a foolish chase away back down the valley of the Don.

But Clyde, as it chanced, came right along, straight for the brood, and Brownie, giving the signal to the children, *'Krrr, krr'* (Hide, hide), ran to lead the man away just as her mate had led the dog. Full of a mother's devoted love, and skilled in the learning of the woods, she ran in silence till quite near, then sprang with a roar of wings right in his face, and tumbling on the leaves she shammed a lameness that for a moment deceived the poacher.

But when she dragged one wing and whined about his feet, then slowly crawled away, he knew just what it meant – that it was all a trick to lead him from her brood, and he struck her a savage blow; but little Brownie was quick, she avoided the blow and limped behind a sapling, there to bat herself upon the leaves again in sore distress, and seem so lame that Clyde made another try to strike her down with a stick.

But she moved in time to balk him, and bravely, steadfast still to lead him from her helpless little ones, she flung herself before him and beat her gentle breast upon the ground, and moaned as though begging for mercy. And Clyde, failing again to strike her, raised his gun, and firing charge enough to kill a bear, he killed poor brave, devoted Brownie.

He knew the young must be hiding near, so looked about to find them. But no one moved or peeped. He saw not one, but as he tramped about with heedless feet, he crossed and crossed again their hiding ground, and more than one of the silent little ones he tramped to death, and neither knew nor cared.

Redruff had taken the yellow cur away off downstream, and now returned to where he left his mate. He found Brownie's scattered feathers, and now he knew the meaning of that shot.

Who can tell what his horror and his mourning were? Some minutes dumbly gazing at the scene, and then suddenly the thought of their helpless brood. He flew to the hiding place at top speed, and called the well known *'Kreet, kreet.'* Did every grave give up its little inmate at the magic word?

No, barely more than half. Six little balls of down unveiled their lustrous eyes, and, rising, ran to meet him; but four did not respond. Redruff called again and again, till he was sure that all who could had come, then led them from that dreadful place, far, far away upsteam, where barbed wire fences and bramble thickets offered more reliable shelter.

Here the brood grew and were trained by their father just as his mother had trained him; though his wider knowledge and experience gave him many advantages. He knew this territory so well, all the feeding grounds, dust baths and safe roosting places, that the summer passed and not a chick was lost.

They grew and flourished and when the Gunner Moon arrived they were a family of six grown-up grouse with Redruff, splendid in his gleaming copper feathers, at their head. He had ceased to drum during the summer after the loss of Brownie, but drumming is to the partridge what singing is to the lark; while it is his love song, it is also an expression of exuberance born of health, and when the molt was over and September food and weather had renewed his splendid plumes, his spirits revived, and finding himself one day near the old log he mounted impulsively, and drummed again and again.

The black grapes and the Migration Moon arrived. But Redruff's brood were of a vigorous stock; their robust health meant robust wits, and though they felt the impulse, it passed within a week and only three had flown away for good.

Redruff, with his remaining three, was living in the glen when the snow came. It was light, flaky snow, and as the weather was not very cold, the family squatted for the night under the low flat boughs of a cedar tree. But the next day the storm continued, it grew colder, and the drifts piled up all day.

By nightfall, the snow had ceased, but the frost grew harder still, so Redruff, leading the family to a birch tree above a deep drift, dived into the snow, and the others did the same. Then into the holes the wind blew loose snow, their pure white bed clothes, and thus tucked in they slept in comfort, for the snow is a warm wrap, and the air passes through it easily enough for breathing. Next morning each partridge found a solid wall of ice before him from his frozen breath, but easily turned to one side and rose on the wing at Redruff's morning *'Kreet, kreet, kwit.'* (Come children, come children, fly.)

This was the first night for them in a snow-drift, though it was an old story to Redruff, and next night they merrily dived again into bed, and the north wind tucked them in as before. But a change in weather was brewing. The night wind veered to the east.

A fall of heavy flakes gave place to sleet, and that silver to rain. The whole wide world was sheathed in ice, and when the grouse awoke to quit their beds, they found themselves sealed in with a great cruel sheet of edgeless ice.

The deeper snow was still quite soft, and Redruff bored his way to the top, but there the hard, white sheet defied his strength. Hammer and struggle as he might he could make no impression, and only bruised his wings and head. The slow hours wore on and found him weakening with his struggles, but no nearer to freedom. He could hear the struggling of his family, too, or sometimes heard them calling to him for help with their long drawn plaintive *'p-e-e-e-e-t-e, p-e-e-e-e-t-e.'*

They were hidden from many of their enemies, but not from the pangs of hunger, and when the night came down the weary prisoners, worn out with hunger and useless toil, grew quiet in despair. At first they had been afraid the fox would come and find them imprisoned there at his mercy, but as the second night went slowly by they no longer cared, and even wished he would come and break the crusted snow, and so give them at least a fighting chance for life.

But when the fox really did come padding over the frozen drift, the deep-laid love of life revived, and they crouched in utter stillness till he passed. The second day was one of driving storm. The north wind sent his snow-horses, hissing and careening over the white earth, tossing and curling their white manes and kicking up more snow as they dashed on. The long, hard grinding of the granular snow seemed to be thinning the snow crust, for though far from dark below, it kept growing lighter.

Redruff had pecked and pecked at the under side all day, till his head ached and his bill was wearing blunt, but when the sun went down he seemed as far as ever from escape. The night passed like the others, except no fox went trotting overhead.

In the morning he renewed his pecking, though now with scarcely any force, and the voices or struggles of the others were no more heard. As the daylight grew stronger he could see that his long efforts had made a brighter spot above him in the snow, and he continued feebly pecking. Outside, the storm-horses kept on trampling all day, the crust was really growing thin under their heels, and late that afternoon his bill went through into the open air.

New life came with this gain, and he pecked away, till just before the sun went down he had made a hole that his head, his neck, and his ever-beautiful ruffs could pass. His great broad shoulders were too large, but he could now strike downward, which gave him fourfold force; the snow crust crumbled quickly, and in a little while he sprang from his icy prison once more free.

But the young ones! Redruff flew to the nearest bank, hastily gathered a few red hips to stay his gnawing hunger, then returned to the prison-drift and clucked and stamped. He got only one reply, a feeble *'peete, peete,'* and scratching with his sharp claws on the thinned granular sheet he soon broke through, and Graytail feebly crawled out of the hole. But that was all; the others, scattered he could not tell where in the drift, made no reply, gave no sign of life, and he was forced to leave them.

Chapter VII
The Gunner Moon

It was a long time before Redruff and Graytail fully recovered, but food and rest gradually restored their strength and spirits, and one bright clear day in midwinter Redruff began to drum on his log once more.

Was it the drumming, or the tell-tale tracks of their snow shoes on the omnipresent snow, that betrayed them to Clyde? He came prowling again and again up the ravine, with dog and gun, intent on hunting the partridges down. They knew when he was there, and he was coming now to know them well. The great copper-ruffed cock was becoming famous up and down the valley. During the Gunner Moon many a hunter had tried to end his life. But Redruff had grown even more wily. He knew just where to hide, and when to rise on silent wing, and when to squat till overstepped, then rise on thunder wing within a yard to shield himself at once behind some mighty tree trunk and speed away.

Clyde never ceased his pursuit but Redruff always found a tree, a bank, or some safe shield between them, and he lived and throve and drummed.

When the Snow Moon came he moved with Graytail to the Castle Frank woods, where food was plentiful as well as grand old trees. There was in particular, on the east slope among the creeping hemlocks, a splendid pine. Its trunk was six feet across, and its first branches began at the tops of the other trees.

This great pine had an special interest for Redruff, now living nearby with his remaining young one, but its base, not its far away crown, concerned him. All around were low, creeping hemlocks, and among them the partridge vine and the wintergreen grew, and the sweet black acorns could be scratched from under the snow. There was no better feeding ground, for when that insatiable gunner came on them there it was easy to run low among the hemlock to the great pine, then rise with a derisive *whirr* behind its bulk, and keeping the huge trunk in line with the deadly gun, skim off into safety.

A dozen times at least the pine had saved them during the lawful hunting season, and here it was that Clyde, knowing their feeding habits, laid a new trap. He sneaked under the bank and watched in ambush while an accomplice went around to drive the birds. The partner came trampling through the low thicket where Redruff and Graytail were feeding, and long before the gunner was dangerously near Redruff gave a low warning *'rrr-rrr'* (danger) and walked quickly toward the great pine in case they had to rise.

Graytail was some distance up the hill, and suddenly caught sight of a new foe close at hand, the yellow cur, approaching fast. Redruff, much farther off, could not see him through the bushes, and Graytail became greatly alarmed.

'*Kwit, kwit*' (Fly, fly) she cried, running down the hill for a start. '*Kreet, k-r-r-r*' (This way, hide) cried the cooler Redruff, for he saw that now the man with the gun was getting in range. He gained the great trunk, and behind it, as he paused a moment to call earnestly to Graytail, 'This way, this way,' he heard a slight noise under the bank before him that betrayed the ambush, then there was a terrified cry from Graytail and the dog sprang at her. She rose in the air and skimmed behind the shielding trunk, away from the gunner in the open, right into the power of the accomplice under the bank.

Whirr, and up she went, a beautiful, soaring creature.

Bang, and down she fell.

It was a perilous place for Redruff. There was no chance for a safe rise, so he squatted low. The dog came within ten feet of him, and the stranger, coming across to Clyde, passed by at five feet, but he never moved till a chance came to slip behind the great trunk away from both. Then he safely rose and flew to the lonely glen by Taylor's Hill.

One by one the deadly guns had struck down his family, till now, once more, he was alone. The Snow Moon passed slowly with many a narrow escape, and Redruff, now known to be the only survivor of his kind, was relentlessly pursued, and grew wilier every day.

It seemed, at length, a waste of time to follow him with a gun, so when the snow was deepest, and food scarcest, Clyde hatched a new plot. Right across the feeding ground, almost the only good one left now in the Stormy Moon, he set a row of snares. A cottontail rabbit, an old friend, cut several of these with his sharp teeth, but some remained, and Redruff, watching a far off speck that might turn out to be a hawk, trod right into one of them, and in an instant was jerked into the air to dangle by one foot.

All that day, with growing, racking pains, poor Redruff hung and beat his great, strong wings in helpless struggles to be free. All day, all night, with growing torture, until he only longed for death. But no one came, until in the last hours of darkness, a great Horned Owl, drawn by the feeble flutter of a dying wing, cut short the pain. The deed was wholly kind.

The wind blew down the valley from the north. The snow-horses went racing over the wrinkled ice, over the Don Flats, and over the Marsh toward the lake, white, for they were driven snow, but on them, scattered dark, were riding plumy fragments of partridge ruffs – the famous rainbow ruffs.

And they rose on the winter wind that night, away and away to the south, over the dark and boisterous lake, as they rode in the gloom, riding and riding on till they were engulfed, the last trace of the last of the Don Valley race.

For now no partridges come to Castle Frank. Its woodbirds miss the martial spring salute, and in Mud Creek Ravine the old pine drumlog had rotted in silence away.

Other Books by Storytellers Ink

A Bug C
Beautiful Joe
Not for Sadie
Black Beauty
Bustop the Cat
Lobo the Wolf
William's Story
Sandy of Laguna
Kitty the Raccoon
The Blue Kangaroo
The Pacing Mustang
The Living Mountain
Cousin Charlie the Crow
The Lost & Found Puppy
If a Seahorse Wore a Saddle
Father Goose & His Goslings
Jasper Jonathan Jeremy Jones
Monica the Monarch Butterfly
Little Annie of Christian Creek
The Adventures of J.G. Cougar
I Thought I Heard a Tiger Roar
Sully the Seal and Alley the Cat
Ragglylug the Cottontail Rabbit
Redruff the Partridge of Don Valley
Tweak and the Absolutely Right Whale